THE CARS AND TRUCKS BOOK

HOT DOGS

ALWAYS FRESH

TODD PARR

Megan Tingley Books

LITTLE, BROWN AND COMPANY

NEW YORK BOSTON

It's another busy day for all the cars and trucks!

Some cars are fast.

Some cars are slow.

Some buses take you to a vacation.

Some buses take you to school.

All cars and trucks LOVE to be on the road!

Some trucks help keep the streets clean.

Some trucks help keep the earth clean.

Some trucks help on the farm.

Some trucks help in the city.

All cars and trucks LOVE to be clean.

Some trucks deliver books.

Some trucks deliver laundry.

Some trucks wash dirty dogs.

Some trucks serve hot dogs.

All cars and trucks LOVE

to help people.

Some trucks haul dirt.

Some trucks play in the dirt.

Some trucks carry trucks.

Some trucks carry ducks.

Some cars like to drive in the snow.

Some cars like to drive to the beach.

to say good night.

Cars and trucks help us do a lot of things. But it's also good to take the bus  or ride a bike.

STOP

SCHOOL BUS

The End. Love, Todd

Always remember to be safe. Stop! Look! Listen!

SAFE DRIVERS SHOULD:

Wear seat belts.

Obey all traffic signs
and lights.

Watch out for pedestrians.

Never eat hamburgers
while driving.

Never speed.

Watch out for animals.

Watch out for bicyclists.

Never bark, growl, or hiss
at anyone.

NEVER text or talk on
their phones.

ALWAYS BE SAFE! Love, Todd

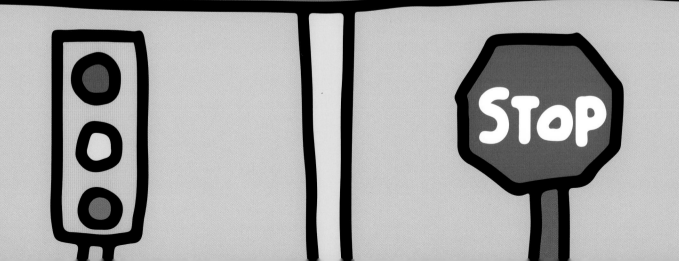

Also by Todd Parr

A complete list of Todd's books and more information can be found at toddparr.com.

About This Book

The art for this book was created on a drawing tablet using an iMac, starting with bold black lines and dropping in color with Adobe Photoshop. This book was edited by Megan Tingley and Russ Busse and designed by Nicole Brown. The production was supervised by Virginia Lawther, and the production editor was Marisa Finkelstein. The text was set in Todd Parr's signature font.

1290 Avenue of the Americas, New York, NY 10104 • Visit us at LBYR.com • First Edition: December 2018 • Little, Brown and Company is a division of Hachette Book Group, Inc. The Little, Brown name and logo are trademarks of Hachette Book Group, Inc. • The publisher is not responsible for websites (or their content) that are not owned by the publisher. • Library of Congress Cataloging-in-Publication Data • Names: Parr, Todd, author, illustrator. • Title: The cars and trucks book / by Todd Parr. • Description: First edition. | New York; Boston: Little, Brown and Company, 2018. | "Megan Tingley Books." | Summary: Illustrations and simple text reveal many things that cars and trucks like to do, from just being on the road to helping keep the planet clean. Includes safety tips. • Identifiers: LCCN 2017051341| ISBN 9780316506625 (hardcover) | ISBN 9780316506601 (ebook) | ISBN 9780316522489 (library edition ebook) • Subjects: | CYAC: Automobiles—Fiction. | Trucks—Fiction. • Classification: LCC PZ7.P2447 Car 2019 | DDC [E]—dc23 • LC record available at https://lccn.loc.gov/2017051341 • ISBNs: 978-0-316-50662-5 (hardcover), 978-0-316-50660-1 (ebook), 978-0-316-50661-8 (ebook), 978-0-316-50659-5 (ebook) • PRINTED IN CHINA • APS • 10 9 8 7 6 5 4 3 2